THE
GRUMPFACE

Cover art and illustrations by D. Frongia

The moral right of the author has been asserted.

Hardback — 978-0-9953592-0-8
Paperback — 978-0-9953592-1-5
Ebook Kindle — 978-0-9953592-2-2
Ebook EPUB — 978-0-9953592-3-9

Published by TaleBlade Press

TaleBlade
www.taleblade.com

For my beautiful wife

THE GRUMPFACE

B.C.R. FEGAN

ILLUSTRATED BY
D. FRONGIA

TALEBLADE

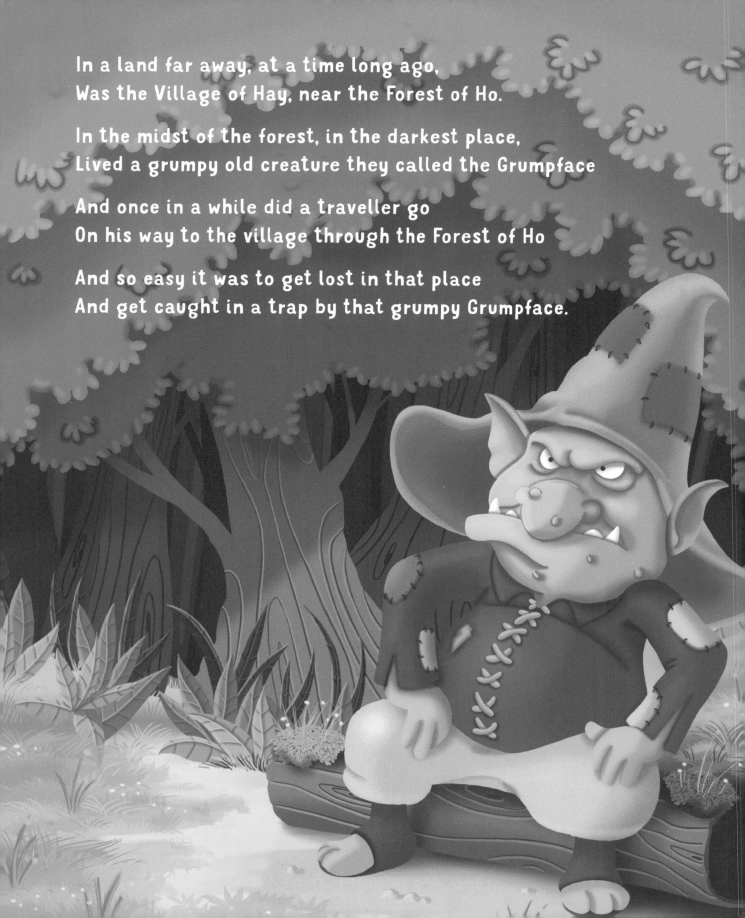

In a land far away, at a time long ago,
Was the Village of Hay, near the Forest of Ho.

In the midst of the forest, in the darkest place,
Lived a grumpy old creature they called the Grumpface

And once in a while did a traveller go
On his way to the village through the Forest of Ho

And so easy it was to get lost in that place
And get caught in a trap by that grumpy Grumpface.

Yet if they could finish one task out of three
The Grumpface would have to let them go free.

For he was cursed long ago, as a grumpy old man
When he grumped at a wizard who came up with a plan

That because he was grumpy and would never replace
His frown with a smile, he'd stay a grumpface.

So there he remained in the Forest of Ho
Spreading his grump wherever he'd go.

In the Village of Hay lived a quiet young man,
An inventor by trade, they called 'Dafty Dan'

For as much as he tried working hard day and night
All his inventions he'd never get right

But still he would try, though he'd end up a mess,
For he'd dreamed that one day a young girl he'd impress.

Yet not just any young girl, you should know
But a beauty named Bella with hair like the snow.

Each day he would see her standing for hours,
Across from his shop, selling her flowers.

He'd hear her sweet voice drift through his door
"I have lilies, violets, daisies and more:

Nightshade, lavender, tulips and rue
I'd sell you a rose but alas, not one grew."

He longed to speak up and make her adore him
But knew if he tried, she'd probably ignore him.

When Dan went to bed and started to doze,
He was struck with a thought — he would
    find her a rose!

He could use his inventions, he'd need about ten
To find her a rose; she would speak to him then.

And so the next morning he made ready to go
And followed his 'finder' to the Forest of Ho

But despite his inventions no rose could be found
And now he was lost, so he sat on the ground.

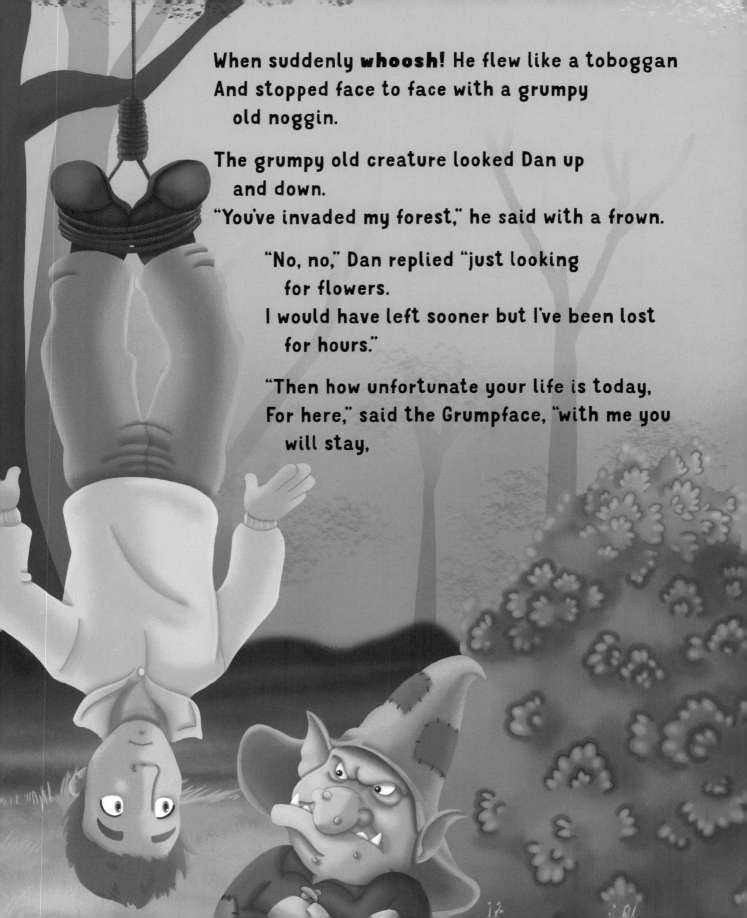

When suddenly **whoosh!** He flew like a toboggan
And stopped face to face with a grumpy
old noggin.

The grumpy old creature looked Dan up
and down.
"You've invaded my forest," he said with a frown.

"No, no," Dan replied "just looking
for flowers.
I would have left sooner but I've been lost
for hours."

"Then how unfortunate your life is today,
For here," said the Grumpface, "with me you
will stay,

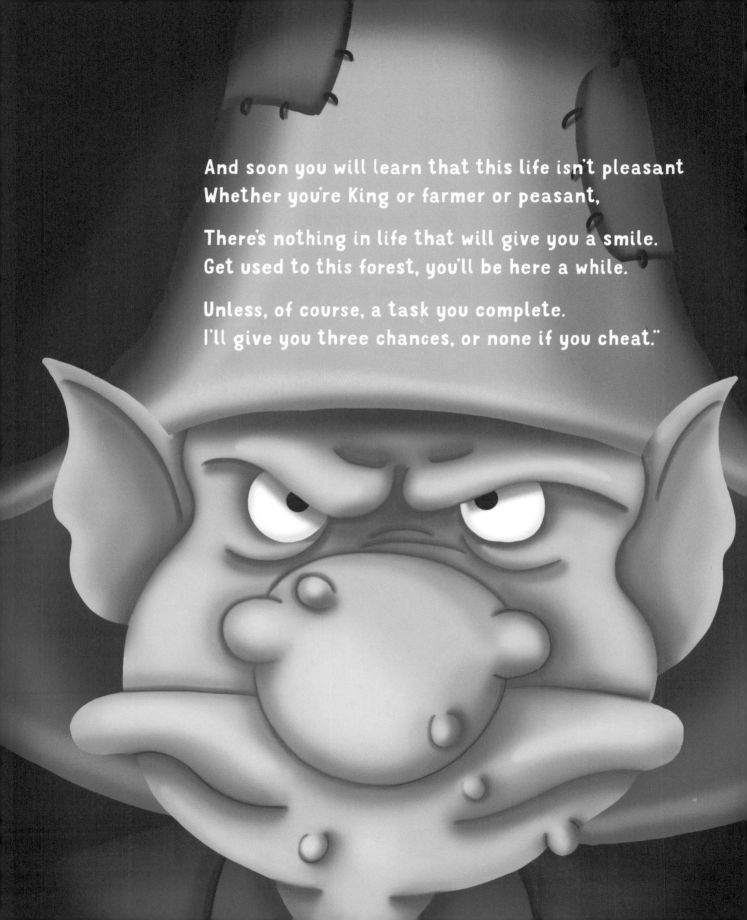

And soon you will learn that this life isn't pleasant
Whether you're King or farmer or peasant,

There's nothing in life that will give you a smile.
Get used to this forest, you'll be here a while.

Unless, of course, a task you complete.
I'll give you three chances, or none if you cheat."

Dan thought of Bella "You don't scare me.
I'll finish a task and then I'll go free.

You're wrong," Dan replied, "that in life you can't grin.
I'll prove that life's pleasant; your task I shall win."

"Hmm!" said the Grumpface. "It's been said in the past.
You're not the first and you won't be the last.

You tell me you're sure that a task you
will win?
Then let us stop talking; let the
challenge begin!

First you must catch me a small,
 glowing bird
That flies like the wind, but never is heard,

And once it is caught, return to this camp
With that small, glowing bird trapped in
 this lamp."

And so Dan began, like nothing was wrong,
For he'd use his inventions to help
 him along.

He pulled out his 'launcher'. His eyes
 gave a flicker.
That bird may be quick but his
 'launcher' was quicker.

Then all of a sudden, as quick as can be,
In front of him perched that bird in a tree.

Steady, he aimed without making a sound;
The lamp launched like lightning, then fell
   on the ground.

"I got it!" Dan cried, as he ran like a champ,
But the bird wasn't caught; she'd swallowed
   the lamp!

"What's this?" The Grumpface appeared behind Dan.
"Has all your hard work gone according to plan?"

"Well, not exactly." Dan's leg gave a stamp.
"Did the lamp catch the bird? No, the bird caught the lamp."

The Grumpface was stunned. It all looked absurd.
There was his lamp inside of the bird!

Dan noticed the mouth of the Grumpface grew wider.
That bird sure looked funny with the object inside her,

But surely the Grumpface could not have been grinning?
His life was all grump, even when he was winning.

His mouth became normal as quick as it grew.
"You've lost," he said quickly, "now, task number two."

He turned and led Dan to a very high peak.
"Across this volcano is the freedom you seek.

Your next task is simple, but you'd better be bold.
You cross by this bridge, but you do it blindfold."

Dan looked at the bridge. It seemed slippery and small.
No sides to hang onto; so easy to fall!

But wait! An invention he had in his sack
Would help him along with the balance he'd lack.

He'd invented some shoes; though they weren't too appealing,
Their grip was so strong he could walk on a ceiling.

Quickly he laced-up the shoes on his feet
And happily walked to the task he would beat.

The Grumpface just grimaced and tied 'round his face
A blindfold, with pins to keep it in place.

"Now walk," said the Grumpface, "you silly young man;
Cross over the lava, let's see if you can."

With his shoes, Dan knew he had made the right choice.
He decided to sing at the top of his voice.

The horrible sound echoed all 'round the ridge.
It dislodged a boulder that fell on the bridge

And as Dan kept singing the bridge was bounced high
And both Dan and the bridge were thrown up in the sky

And as the bridge landed back on the ground,
Dan didn't know it had been flipped around.

So when he had crossed, with joy in his heart,
He threw off the blindfold and . . . was back at the start

And the Grumpface who now seemed a little amused,
Stared wide-eyed at Dan, who was looking confused.

The Grumpface had never seen someone so daft.
His mouth soon grew wide and almost, he laughed,

But quickly, before Dan had noticed his face,
The grump had returned back in its place.

"You lose once again; you will never be free,"
The Grumpface yelled loudly. "To task number three!"

Down from the mountain and straight to a cave.
"For this task," said the Grumpface, "you'd better be brave.

Inside here are dangers from which you can't hide.
Let's see you get to the cave's other side.

But do not come out unless you have found
A small silver statue somewhere on the ground."

Dan racked his brain as he entered the cave.
He had one last invention . . . that didn't behave.

had used it before, when the nights had grown dark.
It was meant to give light: what it gave was a spark.

"Please work," Dan whimpered. "You're all I have now."
CLICK! went the object . . . then suddenly, **WOW!**

A light all around him instantly shone.
"I did it!" Dan shouted, his timidness gone.

Now, with the light, he could dodge all the traps
And jump all the pits and squeeze through the gaps.

While he was carefully making it through
He suddenly saw it: the silver statue.

Proudly he picked up the object with care.
Not much longer and soon he'd be there.

His mind turned to Bella. This adventure he'd tell,
But suddenly: "**Arrghh!**" He tripped and he fell.

Then instantly darkness. The light had gone out.
He'd dropped the small statue, so he fumbled about.

He let out a sigh and lifted his head.
He'd found the small statue and seen light up ahead.

Hurriedly now, he raced to get out.
Clutching the statue, he gave out a shout.

He'd made it! The Grumpface would let him go free.
He'd finished the challenge: task number three!

And there he was now, that grumpy Grumpface,
Looking displeased Dan had walked through that place.

Slowly the Grumpface shuffled to Dan.
He narrowed his eyes. "You've surprised me, young man.

But of course, there is still something left here to do."
Dan smiled proudly and pulled out . . . a shoe?

"Wait!" Dan panicked. "I know it was here."
He searched through his clothes and felt through his gear.

"I . . . I must have dropped it, near the end I fell down."
He felt his own smile turn into a frown.

"Well, I guess I have failed," he said with a sigh,
And under his breath, he said, "Bella, goodbye."

He slowly looked up "A shoe!" Grumpface said.
He suddenly chuckled, then threw back his head.

He let out a laugh so loud and so long
Dan started to wonder if something was wrong.

Then suddenly, **BOOM!** What has
happened, thought Dan.
The Grumpface had changed to
an old, laughing man.

The old man stopped laughing, tears still in his eyes.
"I'm free from the curse." His voice sounded wise.

"Thank you, young man, I have a new start.
You're a clumsy young person, but you have a big heart."

"And now you and everyone else can go free,
Who failed the tasks set sadly by me.

But before I depart, with a smile on my face,
Let me tell you how to get out of this place."

So Dan set out to the Village of Hay
And following directions, stopped off on the way,

And there it was, as the old man had said,
The reward for his help: a rose, coloured red.

And as he returned, he heard her sweet voice,
"If you need some flowers, I'll give you a choice:

Buttercups, poppies, pansies and yew;
I don't have a rose. It's a shame, but it's true."

Slowly Dan walked up to Bella, and froze.
Unable to speak, he held out the rose.

"Oh! Where did you find it?" Bella cried with a smile.
Dan cleared his throat. "It, ah, took me a while."

And with those few words he started his tale,
From the love that he had, to the tasks he would fail.

"But no task was ever as scary as this."
He touched her sweet hand and gave it a kiss.

When he looked up, her smile turned to laughter,
And so they both lived **ungrumpily** ever after.